Chicken Talk

words by
Patricia
MacLachlan
pictures by
Jarrett J.
Krosoczka

KATHERINE TEGEN BOOKS
An Imprint of HarperCollins Publishers

In celebration of chickens and a great rooster
named Winston Churchill . . .
—P.M.

For Joyce, who always read to Gina
—J.K.

Katherine Tegen Books is an imprint of HarperCollins Publishers.

Chicken Talk
Text copyright © 2019 by Patricia MacLachlan
Illustrations copyright © 2019 by Jarrett J. Krosoczka
All rights reserved. Manufactured in China.
No part of this book may be used or reproduced in any manner whatsoever
without written permission except in the case of brief quotations embodied
in critical articles and reviews. For information address HarperCollins
Children's Books, a division of HarperCollins Publishers, 195 Broadway,
New York, NY 10007.
www.harpercollinschildrens.com

Library of Congress Control Number: 2018933258
ISBN 978-0-06-239864-2

Typography by Aurora Parlagreco
18 19 20 21 22 SCP 10 9 8 7 6 5 4 3 2 1
❖
First Edition

Farmer Otis and his wife, Abby, loved their chickens.
Their children, Willie and Belle, loved them, too.

All in all there were eleven hens—

Beatrix
(called Trixie)

Grace

Bitsy

Boo

and the seven white feathered Joyces named after Abby's mother, Joyce, who loved white chickens.

Joyce

Joyce

Joyce

Joyce

Joyce

Joyce

Joyce

There was one colorful rooster named Pedro, who protected his hens from foxes, hawks, and weasels.

Pedro

Abby made them salads with fresh lettuce and arugula from her garden. She collected their eggs in the henhouse.

"Thank you, dear girls," she said as she put the eggs in her basket to sell to the neighbors.

Willie and Belle wrote each hen's name on her eggs—Trixie, Bitsy, Boo, Grace, and the seven Joyces. The neighbors liked that. They had their favorite hens.

Willie and Belle read books under the big tree. The chickens peered and pecked at the books and cocked their heads at Willie and Belle when they told stories.

Every day, Willie let the chickens out of their big pen so they could scratch in the dirt for bugs and worms. They loved being out and about.

While Pedro lurked in the yard watching for danger, the hens sometimes sat on the porch chairs and looked out over the meadow like elegant ladies.

One morning, Willie had a great shock! "Belle!"
he called. "Come quickly!"

Belle ran from the garden.

Willie pointed. "Did you write that?"

Belle looked. She shook her head. In the dirt
they read a message—

No more
ARUGULA

"Maybe Mama wrote it," said Belle. "Or Papa."

Willie shook his head.

"They're at the market," said Willie. "And only
the chickens eat arugula."

Otis and Abby drove into the driveway and walked up the hill with shopping bags.

Willie pointed to the words scratched in the dirt.

Trixie strutted over and looked at Otis and Abby with her bright beady eyes.

"Trixie wrote that sentence," whispered Otis.

"Yes," said Abby.

"Don't tell anyone," said Otis. "They'll think we're nutty."

Abby nodded. "I thought Trixie liked arugula."

When Abby went to collect eggs in the morning, she called, "Another message!"

Otis, Willie, and Belle came running.

The sentence read—

The fox is not intelligent.

Otis looked at Pedro.

"I heard a kerfuffle near the pen last night. Good job, Pedro," called Otis. "I heard your squawking and the flapping of wings. When I came out, the hens were safely in their henhouse and you looked very proud."

"Do you think there will be more chicken talk?" asked Abby.

"Yes," said Otis.

"Yes," said Belle.

And there was.

Willie and Belle found more chicken talk the next day under the tree.

More stories about brave chickens.

"That's Boo," said Willie. "She always has her beak in a book."

"They learned their letters from looking at our stories," said Belle.

Soon the secret came out.

Tripp, the mailman, found a sentence in the dirt by the mailbox.

"Did you write that, Otis?" asked Tripp.

"No," said Otis. "Bitsy did. She's bossy."

"Sounds almost poetic," said Tripp. "Too poetic for a chicken."

"No one in town will believe that your chickens can write. I don't believe it myself."

And the townspeople didn't believe it. How could a chicken write?! Why *would* a chicken write? No other chickens in town wrote messages in the dirt!

"Come see for yourself, Tripp," said Otis. "Put up your tent and spend the night."

Tripp brought his small brown tent and sleeping bag and pillow.
He set up near the chicken yard.

Everyone went to sleep.

There was a full moon.

Early in the morning, while Tripp was still sleeping, Willie let the chickens out of their pen.

In the kitchen, Otis smiled as he drank his coffee. And soon it happened.

Outside there was a loud howl from Tripp.

Otis opened the kitchen door and looked out.

Tripp clutched his pillow, his tent collapsed on one side. He pointed to a message in the dirt.

You snore
and there
is a snake
in your tent.

A small snake slithered off into the
bushes.

"It's true!" said Tripp, trying to catch his
breath. "Who wrote that?"

Pedro walked up to them, his eyes shining.

"I'd say it was Pedro," said Otis.

"And you," said Willie.

Now everyone in town knew about the chicken talk. Being the mailman, Tripp saw everyone. And he told them how he was saved by chicken talk.

Everyone in town bought more eggs and wanted to know the chicken talk of the day.

And there was lots of chicken talk.

too hot.
Can we have a fan?
Much too much rain.
We need an umbrella.

There are new chicks. Come see.

"Has Grace written anything?" asked Abby one day.

"Grace is shy. Maybe she doesn't have anything to say," said Otis.

Grace was Otis's favorite hen. She had golden feathers lined in black. Sometimes the sunlight made her feathers gleam like jewels.

"She is quiet," said Abby. "I like the quiet."

But it wasn't quiet for long.

On Sunday morning, early, there were
seven messages.

Too many Joyces!

I'm the real Joyce.

I'm NOT Joyce.

And not me.

I've never been a Joyce.

I'll never be a Joyce.

No more Joyces.

"What will we do?" said Abby.

"Nothing," said Otis. "They'll tell us."

And they did. Names were found all over the dirt yard.
Willie and Belle discovered them in the driveway and in the
pen and by the barn.

Josie

Louisa May Alcott

Jane The real Joyce

Tripp, again, found one name in the dirt by the mailbox.

"Who's Belinda?" he called.

"One of the Joyces' new names," said Otis.

Mickey

Emily Dickinson

Belinda

And then it was quiet.

"Peaceful," said Otis.

"Papa?" said Willie.

"What?"

"We'll never tell all the white feathered Joyces apart. No matter what they have named themselves."

Otis smiled. "I know. And believe me, they'll tell us."

"More chicken talk," said Belle.

In front of them, scratched in the dirt, were two short sentences.

We love you, good night.

Grace came over to look at them all.

"Grace," whispered Otis. "It was you."

"Grace," said Abby.

"Grace," said Willie and Belle together.

That was the kind of chicken talk they loved.